W9-BPM-664

Anne-Marie the Beauty

Anne-Marie the Beauty

YASMINA REZA

Translated by Alison L. Strayer

Seven Stories Press
New York • Oakland

Copyright © 2019 by Yasmina Reza, Flammarion
English translation © 2021 by Alison L. Strayer

All rights reserved. No part of this book may be reproduced in any form or by any
means, electronic or mechanical, including photocopying, writing or recording, or
through any other system for the storage or retrieval of information without the
written permission of the publisher.

Seven Stories Press
140 Watt Street
New York, NY 10013
www.sevenstories.com

Library of Congress Cataloging-in-Publication Data

Names: Reza, Yasmina, author. | Strayer, Alison L., translator.
Title: Anne-Marie the Beauty / Yasmina Reza ; translated by Alison L.
    Strayer.
Other titles: Anne-Marie la Beauté. English
Description: New York : Seven Stories Press, [2021]
Identifiers: LCCN 2020058082 (print) | LCCN 2020058083 (ebook) | ISBN
    9781644210512 (trade paperback) | ISBN 9781644210529 (ebook)
Classification: LCC PQ2678.E955 A6713 2021 (print) | LCC PQ2678.E955
    (ebook) | DDC 843/.914--dc23
LC record available at https://lccn.loc.gov/2020058082
LC ebook record available at https://lccn.loc.gov/2020058083

Book design by Jon Gilbert

Printed in the USA.

9 8 7 6 5 4 3 2 1

to André Marcon

I come from Saint-Sourd-en-Ger, madame, a place where no one lies about

In Saint-Sourd, when I was a child, there were the coal pits and the Prosper Ginot theater company

You'd see the actors from the Comédie de Saint-Sourd go by in the town square. They walked alone or in pairs

Especially on Sundays, on account of the market

I could always say their names

I murmured them to myself, Armand Cheval, Prosper Ginot, Madeleine Puglierin, Désiré Guelde, Georgia Glazer, Odette Ordonneau

I recognized them all

...

Here I am, cavorting. Almost

Yes...

Will they put my titanium knee joint in the urn after I'm cremated?

I've been wondering

People in the know, madame, say the soul leaves the body right away and you see yourself

You see yourself lowered into the ground

That's why I say cremation

I've had a happy life, you know

My whole knee is titanium, they only left the kneecap

The doctor said, you're almost good as new, you can give the cane a rest

Get that thing out of my sight!

For me a cane means polio

Deformed kids with gimpy legs creeping around Saint-Sourd, hugging the walls

I lived in terror of polio my whole childhood

The slightest twinge and I had polio

Or sometimes it was cancer, or meningitis

But mostly I had polio

I'd never have received you with the cane. You don't mind the slippers?

They're Furlanes

Gondolier slippers from Venice. I have yellow ones too

When my husband was alive, they lay moldering in the closet

He said they made me look stumpy

With the cane, I'd worked out a quiet little circuit with places to sit down on the way to Picard and the Monoprix

And the beauty parlor for my tint

I sat down at the bakeshop with the little tearoom. I sat at the pharmacy, where they like me. Then at Picard, where they adore me. There was the 84 bus stop with a shelter. And an empty cashier's seat at the Monoprix

There are three cashiers for five cash desks. They know me there

At the Monoprix, there's a little evangelical from Madagascar who loves me. Victor. He stacks boxes. He finds whatever I'm looking for

The security guard too—none too swift but nice. He grabs the things I can't reach. I haven't got my range of motion back. They keep the compound for polishing the brass under the shelves for lack of space

That Monoprix's not big enough

They know me there

The new doctor said, you're pretty much good as new, you can ditch the cane

No sooner said than done!

He says my blood pressure's a little high

I said, how's that, doctor, my pressure's high when it never was before? He said, that's how it goes. One day we don't have a thing and the next day we do

I said, *oh là*, I don't care for that way of thinking! Dr. Olbrecht never thought that way

I miss Olbrecht. We knew each other for thirty years

He used to come see me on stage

He took care of my husband and my son too

At a certain age, it's as if word gets round and people slip away on you. The ones who were supposed to be there holding your hand till the end. The doctor, the agent, the husband, my neighbors the Storms

The first time, I saw her through a doorway. Lying on a sofa with all that hair

I'd just arrived in the capital from the North to audition at the Théâtre de Clichy

I saw the bent head at the end of the room with the hair tumbling down. She was smoking

Someone said, that's Giselle Fayolle

I thought she was a big deal, but she was nothing then. Nothing at all

Still, to me a girl with a dressing room in Paris was a big deal

We got to know each other doing *Bérénice*

I played her confidante

In real life too, I sympathized with her lovers

She lived on rue Émile-Augier, and I had a room on rue des Rondeaux which she never visited

When we met again, forty years later, it was still me going to see her

In the end, Giselle had bowel trouble, and I had the buggered knee

We went out to eat from time to time. Or I went to her place on rue de Courcelles

I even slept there once when she was feeling blue

Always me going to see her

After my surgery, I stopped. No more excursions

Of course it was a shock, madame, seeing her there in black and white

Black and white in magazines means six feet under

We were used to seeing that photo in color

Blue sparkles, all the way to her temples

Back then, rumor had it she was Alain Delon's mistress

Maybe Ingmar Bergman's, too

Anyway, tongues wagged

You're at the pedicure salon and turn a page, expecting something frivolous, and there is Gigi Fayolle in black and white

The obituaries below have no photos

I was fresh off the train from Saint-Sourd, in Paris to audition

No one was playing the confidantes in tragedy. I came recommended

When they gave me Phénice, I was so happy, mademoiselle, incredibly, immeasurably happy because of the feeling of luck

Giselle reclined on a flowery sofa with her hair

I was mesmerized by her hair

She was twenty-one. I was nineteen

She was one of those girls who stay in bed till noon and do everything in bed, eat, talk on the phone, read, receive visitors, and in their dressing room they have a sofa, and they lie down again with their feet up

That was Giselle when I knew her. Lying with a cup of tea and a biscuit within reach

She had a room on Rue Emile Augier, near La Muette. Mine was on rue des Rondeaux in the 20th

The street faces the wall of Père Lachaise cemetery. What a view. Like a bullet in the head. I've never understood people who can eat just one biscuit. One biscuit, where's the joy?

She snapped up all the big roles. By lying on her back like a sleeping statue on a tomb, and looking as if there was nothing in the world that she wanted. She got all the queen roles, the madwomen, the whores, and even the colonial floozies. It's good for your career to look as if you don't want anything

I gave languor a try, too

But not everyone is cut out for languor

Dr. Olbrecht threw parties at his home, with themes. One year it was the desert and the Bédouins. He called a special events planner. He ordered a lorry-load of sand and a multicolored tent. They sat around the living room, Bédouin-style, the doctor's wife eating dates with their friends on ten inches of sand

I was a little sweet on Olbrecht

His wife up and left him, just like that. What is good for a woman?

I had a nice husband. Uncomplicated

His pet activity was repainting the apartment

He always wanted to repaint, repaint, repaint. He was wild about making things fresh again

I was bored with my husband, but you know, boredom is part of love

He talked to me about his expert appraisals in termite control. We played Scrabble

He was a hundred percent organized, he could not bear the unforeseen

My husband could not survive without structure. Even a penal structure would have suited him. Electroshock at five, torture at half past six. Those are the rules, so we know what we're doing. I'd have been content to play la Bédouine with Olbrecht

You play la Bédouine and when you're a widow, you end up in a hole in the wall with a hot plate and your heap of trinkets

My husband left me two pension and retirement protection plans, plus two life insurance policies in my name. Not to mention a nice three-room flat, a stone's throw from Place Pereire

But the specter of the wheel that turns is never far

You start out as little people, and you're little people in the end

Gigi received her lovers slathered in beauty masks and while shaving her legs. She made her own masks from vegetables, aubergines, carrots

She had no intellectual life whatsoever

If you ask me, she never read a whole play, not even the ones she acted in

For *Bérénice*, she only read her own scenes

The playbill was posted at the entrance to the theater. My name was at the bottom. I passed it sixty times a day. I walked up and down rue du Calvaire to test the effect of the name Anne-Marie Mille on people passing by. It was in small letters at the bottom, next to last, but you could see it clearly because of the double space just below. The name caught your eye. Especially on the downhill walk

Anne-Marie Mille had the ring of stardom

Who's playing in *Three Sisters*? . . . Anne-Marie Mille. Anne-Marie Mille!

Who's playing Angélique? . . . Anne-Marie Mille. Anne-Marie Mille, *magnifique*!

My life was a near miss, madame. In some of the photos from Saint-Sourd, I have the hands of a girl in a coma. Arms dangling, wrists curled, fingers pointing upward. I saw on TV that when a person in a coma curls his wrists, he's a goner

We gave poetry recitations at the youth club hall of the church, and people said, Anne-Marie's diction is excellent, Anne-Marie has perfect enunciation

I did enunciate well

I enunciated well because I loved to say the words, mademoiselle

Words expanded me

On weekends and holidays, they made me wear white gloves like American women

I did not know how to hold myself in the bulky old-lady dress and the hairstyle they'd given me

Parted down the middle

The natural wave flattened on top, with kisscurls at the sides. I already had breasts

She cut my hair all the time, all the time

My mother was a laundress at the Hôtel du Quai. She'd started as a worker in the lace mills. In the blank where you wrote your parents' occupations, I had to write *pattern maker*

She killed herself two or three times a year

At thirteen, I made myself hairpieces from synthetic yarn to have the feel of bouncy locks on my cheeks

They were supposed to make me look pretty, mademoiselle

My mother said, we need to see her face, but my face was not right

They worked on straightening and styling the hair, but my face never followed

The stiff white dress with puffy shoulders

Diamond-patterned tights

I felt hideous, hideous

I can spot an unhappy girl in her Sunday best from ten miles away

When an actor from Saint-Sourd passed, we stopped to look. Afterward the street seemed empty

They were tall and pale. They walked above the ground with graceful strides We couldn't hold a candle to them

The new generations will never witness this procession. Never, monsieur

It snowed last night. Real snow. The bus shelter is completely covered

My son told me, a woman your age took a migrant into her home and he knifed her

Right . . .

My son bought me a blood pressure monitor

I made the mistake of telling him the new doctor thinks my blood pressure's high

Who wants that kind of thing around? I chucked it in the cupboard with the cane

He's a worrier. A worrier like his father

Advice, advice, advice

He has a new tic. He clears his throat on the phone. He

clears it every two sentences. I say, if you're phoning just to clear your throat, don't bother

When he comes to the house, I bring out the blood pressure cuff. I leave it lying around as if I used it. The sight of those medical gewgaws makes my skin crawl. They spell the end

He's barely in the door when he says, it's an oven in here! I say, I like it this way. —It's eighty degrees! I can't stay in this kind of heat. —Well, go, then! It's my home and I'm fine. I have to grab him before he fiddles with the dials on the boiler. Why must you take control of everything against my will? —Someone has to keep an eye on you. You exhibit disturbing behavior. Wanting to be warm is a disturbing behavior?

That's how it is with us, the world shrunk down to the strictest run-of-the-mill

If I ask about his life, he gets all worked up. We only talk about my woes, never anything of interest. He goes to the kitchen and lines up my boxes of prescriptions in a row so I don't mix them up

I say, what's the point? Your grandmother—my mother—had a plastic bag full of pills she nibbled at like Haribos.* She just dug in, not knowing what she was taking

---

* Haribos : sweets made by the German confectionary company Haribo, whose numerous varieties are widely distributed—and very popular—in France.

And look how she ended up

Dead, same as everyone else. Who has it any better in the end?

I almost forgot an important detail, madame: I started with cut-out pictures of Brigitte Bardot

My mother brought home old magazines from the hotel. She flipped through them at night, sipping a Gypsy Rose. She powdered herself like a corpse and went full tilt on the rouge. I never knew if it was due to bad lighting over the sink, or because she was a nutter

In the magazines, I always looked for photos of Brigitte Bardot. I clipped them out and pasted them in an album that I showed to invisible visitors

I narrated episodes from my life, turning the pages with modesty because of course this beauty was me. Anne-Marie the Beauty

I posed with thigh-high boots like Nancy Sinatra, and pulled funny faces on a boat in Norway

Sometimes I told my visitors, yes you're right, I do look pensive sitting on that bench. It was a dark time of my life

But I didn't talk about my beauty or my hair

Or I just said, yes, a French twist is the height of chic! I like to do my hair that way once in a while

Giselle never had hair like Brigitte Bardot's. No!

I spoke loudly in a voice that was not mine. I was

always afraid someone would hear or see me. Our room was a hallway. You could enter through two diagonal doors. We had a trundle bed. My sister slept on the lower shelf, which was never properly raised off the floor. For her entire childhood, she slept low to the ground. In the daytime, her bed disappeared. It ticked me off when she sat on mine. Sometimes I gave her a push. People would yell at me. They said, where do you expect the poor thing to sit? Poor thing! Always *the poor thing*

Anne-Marie the beauty did not have a bedroom with daisy-patterned walls. Anne-Marie the beauty was beautiful, her hair wasn't parted down the middle, or set in an ugly perm, or flat as a pancake at the top of her head and puffed-out around the ears

She was an unknown, you know

She lived in the North too

You can't exactly say Giselle's death made waves. Anyway, that's how it seems to me

What did I read? ... *Paris Match*, the tabloids ...

On TV? ... They showed a repeat of *The False Lovers*, it was the least they could do ... Other than that?

I don't follow all those social networks. Maybe people talked more about her there

I appreciate your coming to interview me

One thing you must never forget, madame. In our world, we fall from on high

In theaters, back in the old days, artists took up a collection for comrades in need

A woman in a crinkly red dress gave a half-pious, half-menacing speech, then went around with her money-box

She exhaled bad luck. A lopsided hairdo, kind of ratty

A hairdo where you twist the strands and pin them up for volume, and it all collapses on one side. That's the bad-luck hairdo

Other times, to cheer things up, there was a man with a D'Artagnan hat

They called out names you'd seen on playbills, once upon a time, poor folk who believed their star had risen

You wait a long time for your turn to come, and it may even happen, a flash in the pan, before the wheel goes round and turns you into a shadow. Living in a hole in the wall with a hot plate, and your baubles and lace

Marguerite Orsoni fell to earth with a crash

Those swaggering Barnums ...

They all fell with a crash

The specter of the wheel that turns is never far

You know the old joke? A man goes to a psychic. She tells him, don't worry, the wheel is turning and your troubles are over. The man leaves happy, crosses the street, and a car runs him down

Well, at least I'm laughing ... Where were we?

Gigi did not end up in a hole in the wall ... But you

know, madame, alone in a big apartment where there's not the faintest sound, and everything is calcifying...

On rue de Courcelles, there was a camphor smell as soon as you got in the door. She smeared that old Elizabeth Arden eight-hour cream all over herself. I said, Gigi, you reek of camphor. She answered it's an aphrodisiac. Poor thing

In the days of the Théâtre de Clichy, I was her only friend. All the other girls were jealous

Men swarmed around her like flies. She fell in love a few times a month. At twenty-three she fell pregnant. For two days, we racked our brains for what to do, and then she said, enough, I'm keeping it. She had no interest in knowing who the father was. He'd just get up my nose, she said

We were performing *Ondine*. The wardrobe mistress let out Gigi's dress at the seams. We only broke for a month, around the time she gave birth

She had Corinna. Corinna Fayolle, nicknamed Kikine back then. The same girl who showed up at the funeral in a culotte skirt fifty years later

I remember Giselle's parents, madame. They cowered in the hospital room as if they were in the way. I had never seen them before. When they came to the theater, they left right after. The mother finally took her coat off, on orders from Gigi, but kept it folded over her arm, as if they were in some official place. From time to time, Gigi's mother sent Kikine nice little smiles, but from too far away. They were compact, tidy people. You sensed they weren't rolling in dough. Anyway, no one then was rolling in dough

We never talked about our parents except to run them down

Hers seemed inoffensive to me. Paragons, compared to mine

Whatever else they were, they could be trusted to take care of Kikine. I would not have left my son with my mother for even an hour. Besides, she couldn't care less about him

It tore her apart that I wanted to act

Maybe she'd wanted that destiny for herself

She told me, it's hard to be an actress, you need to have the calling. Does she have the calling? Do you have the calling, Anne-Marie? —Yes I have the calling —Since when have you had the calling? —Since always, what do you mean by "calling"? —See? She has no idea what she's talking about! Having the calling means knowing you have it. Your sister doesn't want to act, but at least she has the looks

I had pimples. She gave me some kind of goo from her medicine chest, a tinted paste called Acnomil that was supposed to smother them. My chin looked thicker and of a different color than the rest of my face

Corinna was part of the troupe. She was the nicest baby

on earth, even after she began to walk and babble. Kikine and I were part of the troupe. I say that, mademoiselle, because I was not the kind of person that a group would ordinarily adopt. The neighborhood girls in Saint-Sourd played elastics and skipped rope in the long narrow park just behind our place. I stood watching and was almost never asked to join in. If ever I was, I could not breathe for joy

Giselle changed nothing about her way of life. She remained indolent. Still lounged about with her long tumbling hair and cigarettes. She did children's jigsaw puzzles and made collages with the little girl

There was always someone around to take care of her

When I had my son, I was a bundle of phobias and terrors, and I remembered how relaxed Giselle had been

What's more, she was relaxed about everything. Her relaxation was all-inclusive. At some point in her life, she went to see a shrink, who claimed she did not show enough interest in other people. Gigi told him, if I hear you say "the rich world of the other" once more, I'll belt you one. The shrink was horrified, really, Giselle, is that any way to talk?

The shrink could not come to grips with the likes of Giselle Fayolle

His lamebrain grids were not designed for that type of animal. I say this affectionately, monsieur

Raymond Lice played Argan in *The Imaginary Invalid*,

and wanted nothing to do with la-di-da stage directions. All the Argans and Orgons and Orontes, he said, are prehistoric types. Civilization landed on them like a ton of bricks, but they don't understand a thing about it. Scratch below the surface and you'll see, they are straight out of prehistory, genetically primitive

Just like Giselle, Marietti, a hateful communist woman, once said

Gigi laughed. She agreed

It was a happy time

The world wasn't going to hell in a handcart, the way it is today. You threw a beer can out the window, you didn't give a hoot

Sometimes I got in a real funk, back on rue des Rondeaux

Rue des Rondeaux was more than I could take. Not even because of the graveyard or the wall but because of how far it was from everything, out on the fringes

No one came to visit rue des Rondeaux

It was as if I'd landed back in the place I was from, but even more alone

I'd fixed up a nice, orderly room for myself, with a set of shelves where I put my theater books. I had an easy chair

Sometimes, sitting on my bed, I didn't know where I was anymore, more lost in that simple decor than in the depths of the forest

Prosper Ginot never went up to Paris. None of the

actors from the Comédie de Saint-Sourd ever went to Paris to make a career. Not Armand Cheval, nor Odette Ordonneau

If you had seen their majesty, madame

No Paris actor ever had that majesty, no

It's true that my behavior is disturbing. The other day I threw my glasses in the garbage bin, and yesterday I opened the fridge with an oven mitt to grab a jar of stewed apples

That didn't happen when my husband was around. Or not much. I was more alert. He wasn't a man to laugh at that sort of thing

When he woke up, his coffee cup had to be positioned on the little shelf of the machine, the coffee pod inserted, all ready to go, so he only had to push the button. Believe it or not, it gave me pleasure. I liked preparing his morning routine

I miss my husband

We all have our little manias

I'm old now. It's important to have a hand to grab onto

But mind, I'm not being sentimental. I've never been the sentimental kind. Well, yes, I used to be, unfortunately, but in secret and without all the claptrap that goes with it

I would have loved to play Elvire. Giselle played her. Very badly. In the middle of the run, she left to shoot a film. She was replaced by a wretch of a girl with a high-pitched voice. If you ask me, a high-pitched voice in theater should be like flat feet used to be in the army: you're out on your ear. End of story

Giselle had no understanding of the lament, the universal nature of the lament

You can't ask an indolent person to understand anything about it

She went from rageful to tremulous

Stony, with the inflections of a religious fanatic

Whereas in *Elvire* you have to arrive on stage with a sword and knightly armor

I would have done a good job of it, madame…

Any man who hears this lament should capitulate, no matter how debauched he is. Any man who doesn't is a brute. That Don Juan is a real son of a bitch. I could never stand to look at him in paintings

Giselle left us high and dry. She decamped mid-run, snapped up by the movies

Overnight, we became people of no account. She dropped in on the fly to collect her things or smooth the feathers of her replacement, her cheeks on fire, always in a hurry to leave. We were the go-nowhere people, the little neighborhood troupe unraveling, bit by bit, into oblivion

It pained me not to see Corinna anymore. I loved that kid. I made her dressup clothes from costume remnants. We played rock paper scissors

I asked Giselle to let her stay with me once in a while. But she had moved on to another life

Shouldn't feel sorry for oneself

On stage, you leave nothing behind. The stage doesn't given a damn who occupies it, Giselle, Giselle Fayolle, Anne-Marie. There's nothing left of anyone, not an odor or a shadow

I had a happy life you know

I didn't have the figure for the movies

Giselle had a dressing room. She was the only one who had her own dressing room. When they emptied it, all that was left was the flowery daybed, always heaped with clothing, shawls, underclothes, her kimonos. Gigi was hopelessly messy

All that was left was the daybed she was lying on the first time I saw her, where she smoked and primped her life away

When I think back to the Théâtre de Clichy, the image of that piece of furniture returns, all alone in the room with nothing on top of it

Now that I have nothing to do, monsieur, I thought time would lie heavy on my hands. It's just the opposite, the days and nights gallop along so fast it makes me dizzy

Literally dizzy

All the same, there's nothing normal about opening the fridge with an oven mitt

My mother was half nuts. I wonder if I might be following suit

I already have some of her quirks

I collect light bulbs, I keep empty bottles

In the evening I crunch on orange and lemon Ricola drops to make little pieces. I make a dozen pieces and put them in a cup by my bed, and I crunch some more when I'm under the covers, between sips of herbal tea

It bores me just to suck them

She did the same with Vichy pastilles*

My mother could not look at herself in a mirror without putting on a face, though she was a pretty woman. Even in shop windows. The slightest hint of a reflection, and out came the face. She thrust her chin forward, making her mouth a bitter line while curving her lips up a little at the corners to compensate

Now I do it too. I've seen myself. I thrust out my lower jaw as soon as I spot a mirror

I couldn't stand to see her do it, but I do the same thing

Apparently it's quite common

From time to time, she gamboled home down rue Chelles, rue Carmelin, the nasty little streets near our home

---

* Vichy pastilles : Produced since 1825, these octogonal pastilles are made from mineral salts from the Vichy waters, mint-flavored and traditionally thought to aid digestion.

I don't like nutters

Better to shoot me dead

When we were playing *The Moods of Marianne*, I had a lover Giselle knew

He took me to a place with dark exposed beams and we ate paupiettes. Then we went back to his furnished room, where he dressed me up as Jacqueline Huet, a newscaster from the sixties. He had the jewelry, the string of pearls, the blouse with the pussycat bow, the whole kit and kaboodle. He also had a blonde wig, but I did not want to wear it. We covered my black hair with a chiffon scarf. Next, he declared his love, using the polite form of address, *vous*, and calling me Jacqueline. Then he pounced. I had orders to fend him off. I could scratch, hit, and bite, and we smacked each other's faces until he gave the signal, and Jacqueline had to surrender, in spite of herself

Afterwards, things simmered down, he called me a telly slut, a whore and so on

... but he was nice about it

We got along well

He was a leather salesman

He never wanted me to be any other woman but Jacqueline Huet

And then he went back to Brest, where he came from

Before my husband, I had several lovers. But I became attached too quickly

There was one who drove a Matra-Simca, with room for three in front. He drove at breakneck speed, lying on the seat with the steering wheel at arm's length. It was his coming-up in the world

He could not bear to be contradicted. If I made the mistake of saying Oh Serge be careful! he'd say What??! and his chin muscles would clench and go wobble-wobble, and it was obvious he'd be sulking for at least three months

I lacked lightness. My body was light but not my thoughts

You know, mademoiselle, with men it is good to be beautiful on the outside but inner beauty is never good

I say that in all seriousness because it's a serious matter

Giselle had loads of suitors because she had the heart of an artichoke

After the show, we went out for drinks with people from the theater. Then some went home and we moved to another bar. Later we went somewhere else again. The other girls went home to bed. We could do four or five places a night. What's a person looking for, going from bar to bar like that?

I haven't a clue what we talked about. Nothing. Not much happened. By the end the only ones left were drunks, sent packing by the hookers on the boulevard

I sat tight

I wasn't in anyone's way

People smoked. I thought about life. The night sounds were soothing, the zinc bar, the loud voices

What have you got to lose by sitting around bored, monsieur?

One day my father fled to a resort in the South of France

We didn't have much to do with him. He always came home late, planted his hands on either side of his plate, and said, who's the boss around here? —You are. —What am I? —You're the boss, papa. My mother would say, where would we be without a boss?

That's right!

He couldn't care less about subtleties

He absconded one day in October. We only found him because he bounced a check, or I don't know what. I went with my aunt to bring him back

When we got there, he was lying alone in an enclosed space with a swimming pool in the middle, no greenery, surrounded by white bars

We saw him through the bars. He lay on a deck chair which faced the opposite direction from all the other deck chairs that lay empty. His body massive, feet apart. In a black swimsuit, dark glasses, and cowboy hat. On a huge striped towel

I had never seen my father's body, I mean not really

Certainly not lying down, idle

Where I come from, the lying-down position is good for one thing: pushing up daisies. And how!

After a while, he got up and entered the water, the way old people do, in the shallow end. Chest back, knees slightly bent, forearms floating horizontally

My father made no attempt to swim but stayed put, bobbing in the water with his white hat

We waited for him to come out but he did not come out

You mustn't believe it was common, monsieur, to drift along in life, not in our neck of the woods. You had to be bold

Before we left, he wanted to show us the sea. It was a seaside resort, I forget the name. We walked down the beach, past the campsite, with my aunt, my father's sister. The beach was almost empty. There were just a few people with mini-umbrellas, mostly alone. We passed a couple in their sixties wearing loud Hawaiian shirts. The man was fat, he hurled a piece of wood a few feet for a dog that fetched it, over and over. My dad said, that mutt's a real dolt. He still wore his cowboy hat. I don't know where he'd got it from. I thought, they must all tell themselves the same baloney, these oldsters in their tropical and Wild West getups. They thought of themselves as living outside landscape. They didn't give a hoot about the rinky-dink beach, off-season

Meanwhile back in Saint-Sourd, my mother had committed suicide

A little vein slashed in the bathroom, a slapdash job, so my sister would get to her in time

She was not used to my father getting himself talked about. She took great pains to be the center of everything, the single joy of her misery. The beach escapade with all the fuss and worry made her blood boil

Wanting to be elsewhere was her specialty. Since when did others want to be someplace else? I never understood what kept those two together

Anyway, we should never look too closely at our parents' marriage. And what couple should we look at closely, mademoiselle?

By the time I met my husband, I was done with all my attempts at love's bliss that never came to anything

My mother never forgave my father his extravagant escape

Not long after, I told her I was taking singing lessons. She laughed and laughed as if she had never heard anything so ludicrous. But Anne-Marie, you're such a bad singer! —That's just it —You've never had an ear. Always looking for attention! Now I've heard it all! ... And with what money, pray tell? —It's free. —What has possessed you, when did this start? This whole family is ganging up to push me over the edge. I can't take any more! I've got myself some cyanide

After her second child, Giselle returned to theater

We didn't see each other but I kept track of her career

I said to my husband, let's go, I'll introduce you. Naturally I had told him about the days of our youth

She was playing in *Break of Noon* at the Metropolis*

We were not allowed backstage. We had to wait for her downstairs in an overheated little room with the other second-class citizens. I had gained weight. I wasn't sure she would recognize me right away

Giselle was at the height of her glory, madame

After a long wait, we heard her voice in the stairway. She appeared in a purple coat, her arms full of flowers. There were a lot of people. It was difficult to get close to her. We were ill at ease. My husband did not understand why I was so shy. He whispered, go on, show yourself... At a certain point, she moved toward the exit. I said, Gigi?... What happened next was wonderful, monsieur. She turned and said, Anne-Marie!... Anne-Marie, darling!

She hugged me, which she had not done with any of the others waiting in the lobby. Right away I asked about Kikine. She was thirteen. No one called her Kikine anymore. Giselle remembered rock paper scissors and the little tyke traipsing around backstage, cutting imaginary objects with her fingers. I congratulated her on her new baby girl. We talked about old times, Mireille Camp, Raymond Lice. And Poupi Canella who'd made a career

---

* *Break of Noon* (*Partage du midi*), a play by Paul Claudel (1905).

in vaudeville. I introduced my husband. She said to the people around us, this is Anne-Marie Mille! We were at the Clichy together!

On the way back my husband said, you didn't tell her you have a son. I said, oh, that's true. —You should have told her you had a son. —Yes, you're right, I didn't have time

But I was happy, you see, because she remembered our little theater, our friendship

I said to my husband, see how glad she was to see me? He said, she may have been glad, but she made no effort to see you again, did she? —So? Neither did I. We have separate lives now

People who aren't in the business cannot understand. I said to my husband, you didn't have to shove your neck out like a guinea fowl to say hello. How do you think that made me look, me and my petrified husband?

After meeting her that time, I looked for recent photos of Kikine in the papers. I found an article with a picture of the new family posing on a garden swing. Giselle, José Valadi, their baby Lola, and Kikine

I mean Corinna

Corinna was nothing like Kikine. Everything Kikine had been, the pudgy-cheeked little imp whom I dressed up as a proper lady or a little match girl (she liked playing the little orphan girl), everything that Kikine had been was gone

At thirteen, childhood's over, end of story

She stood apart from the others in a display of boredom and disgust, with spiky hair and lipstick. A stuck-up little queen with none of her mother's dazzle, completely full of herself

At seventeen, she high-tailed it to Mexico with a drug trafficker

I only say this because it's a well-known fact. Everyone knows that Corinna Fayolle ran off with a gangster

With his big mouth, José Valadi looked like Tony Curtis

Now he's little Mister Average. Except for his hair color. It was jet black then and now it's jet black Plus. I saw him at the funeral. He gets invited on TV to comment on soccer

I see life as a great arc. You raise yourself up and when you come back down, you return to your original form, shrunken, head hung low

I went to see my sister at Rangé-sur-Mer. Had to take the cane because you can't get down to the platform on those rickety steps, thirty feet off the ground. The lady inspector comes by and sees me in the vestibule between two carriages. I've been there since Amiens, the train only stops at Rangé for three minutes, so I have to get ready ahead of time. I say, madame, when I was twenty, I was quite the athlete, but time takes its toll... instead of saying, goddammit, woman, give me a hand down!

I played Clytemnestra, mademoiselle, at an age when I was not yet a mother in real life

Raymond Lice was Agamemnon

Raymond Lice as Agamemnon was madness, complete absurdity. Raymond Lice, who always smelled of onions, playing the king of Mycenae! I told him he reeked of onions, and he said give me a mint instead of carping! No, Raymond, you need more than a mint, it's your esophagus the problem. He was peeved that I'd criticized his digestion. Raymond was forty years older than the rest of us. His head sat directly on top of his torso. I had a Grecian coiffure, crimped with ribbons in a great rippling tower on top of my head. In the fourth act, I threw myself at his feet, discreetly removing a hairpin, and all the supernatural curls of the wig spilled down over my shoulders, face, and back. I tossed my head, and made them tremble all over. I put on a voice, at once breathless and inflamed, and Raymond did his cavern voice, and we were the Beauty and the king of the empire

On stage I was sometimes Anne-Marie the beauty

Yes, mademoiselle

Yes, child

Sometimes, we think we're doing quite well, and some little thing proves it's just the opposite

My son comes over. He sits down in front of the evening news

I don't dare tell him that I just got fleeced by one of

those fake EDF guys who came to replace my electrical panel

My son takes a packet of Pépito biscuits from the cupboard and wolfs them down one after the other

He's gone bald at the back of his head. He's running to fat

The concierge makes him gingerbread cookies. She brings them in a confectioner's bag with little pictures on it. I tell her, he's forty-two years old, Madame Mehmeti!

Women never stay with him for long. Or else he's the one who loses interest. Who's to know? I've stopped asking

For a time he lived with a Basque girl who played the accordion. My husband was happy. He already saw himself in his dotage, playing pétanques with the in-laws in Saint-Jean-Pied-de-Port

I say, it's stupid to fill up on sweets. I'll cook you dinner, if you want. He says he doesn't have time. If I dare comment on the news, he says, shh, let me watch

Anyway, what do I care

I don't see what could save us from ruin now, monsieur, civilization is a washout. The only place where air pollution has declined is in the Middle East. Why? Because of war. Fewer cars, less hairspray. When Man is killed off, Nature takes a turn for the better. If the heads of state want to fix all that by fisticuffs, I have no objection

When the weather report comes on, I admit to my son
that I've been billed two thousand euros to have the electrical panel changed

—Are you crazy? Who did you call?! —EDF, the number
is in my address book… —Show me the quote… "Artisanal
Service"? Where do you see Électricité de France? I said, the
fellow was nice, he phoned his boss in front of me. —Of
course he did, and the boss said, lay it on thick, give the old
bag a nice fat quote! Why didn't you phone me? You call four
times a day to ask the name of a singer for your crossword,
then you sign three postdated checks all by yourself?!

When he's gone, I cry

Children do not keep a person warm for long

A little in the early years

He's a devil. I want nothing more to do with him

Soon I can return to acting

Olbrecht would have had me back on stage in the bat
of an eye

Back to normal after the summer, the new doc says.
That's the way they do things now. Zero risk

He thinks I should lose weight

He's a comedian!

I've had a few offers these past weeks, if you can
imagine!

I said, I'm on my way, darlings, if you don't mind the
crutches

Do you know what my dream role is, monsieur? Mary Cavan Tyrone in *Long Day's Journey into Night*

Or the Great Blackbird in *The Bright Red Bird*

Or Arkadina. Same as every actress

Or Lady Prior in *Henry XV*. I'm too old to play her now, though I played Clytemnestra at the age of twenty-seven, monsieur, younger than my daughter Iphigenia, but we can't go back in time, only forward

Mary Tyrone talks about her hair the moment she feels she is being watched. My mother did the same. Always the hand in the hair to fix the styling, flutter over the flat spots, replace the barrettes. I do it too

All these women fretting over their hair when you look at them too hard

We should give this some thought

I miss Olbrecht. I had a soft spot for Olbrecht. I wonder if I might have invented a few aches and pains just to see him

Did he have a soft spot for me?

When I left his office, I'd hear him through the door, saying the name of the next patient in his abrupt, familiar voice. Right away, I felt a pang of abandonment. Did he tell them about his miniature cities and theme nights too? Monsieur, when a woman is in love, she bends over backwards, she dithers about, and runs herself ragged, while men quietly remain themselves

Where is he now? Where does he live?

Maybe he's alone like me. He owned a farmhouse in the Bordeaux Landes that he'd been fixing up for years

When anyone asked, how are you, doctor? he would answer, by definition, well, and probably quite well in reality, too

People say the happiest lives are the least eventful

I should think about buying my funeral urn

An elegant brass model, discreetly engraved, like Poupi Canella's

My son will make a beeline for the cheapest one, and it will be shabby

I do not want to end up in a shabby container

My ashes will fly away to the North

May they be scattered over the chicory fields near Saint-Sourd, or in the Bay of Somme with the dolphins

Poupi had hers scattered on her first love's gravestone, like icing sugar

She'd had her funeral dress picked out for years. Pink silk organdy with a plunging neckline trimmed in rhinestones, waiting at the bottom of a closet, in a plastic garment bag that stank of mothballs

When we took the dress out, we could have fit four Poupis inside. Not to mention the look of a plunging neckline on an emaciated chest butchered by a tracheotomy. I said, Poupi cannot be laid out in this getup. Let the undertakers do their job, her daughter said. So Poupi, the next time we saw her, lay in her coffin, stuffed and wizened from head to toe, with purple lips, her face and hair straight out of a flour barrel, and a Breton shawl wound around her chest

Her children, the priest, everyone leaned over this cradle with compunction

As for me, madame, I had such an irrepressible urge to laugh that I had to escape

I went out in the hall and felt Poupi beside me, happy I was laughing, happy I was applauding her last performance

She had done this all her life. She played Mother Ubu, Madame Sans-Gene, left entire music halls in stitches with Cabrioche. She played in vaudeville, dressed in the most outrageous outfits

Poupi Canella wanted to hear people laugh

Well, course I've gained weight

Nice of you to say so, doc!

Weeks of dragging myself between home and Picard with my cane

I went to the BHV to buy an electronic scale. I saw a black one, very classy, the salesman boasted that it could also calculate my body mass index... Right

On my way out, I passed La maison de la truffe, absurdly located on the same floor as the scales. I looked at condiments, honey, mozzarella with truffle oil on sale, I told myself well no, of course not! Then I saw jars of black truffle cashew nuts that made me think right away of the cashews infused with truffle oil at Saint-Julien des Vignes, a divine combination, monsieur, for people like me, who are mad for cashews and truffles, my two great loves, along with avocadoes. I got home with the scale and two jars of cashews, one of which I had completely emptied by dusk with a small glass of Meursault, watching silent images of people singing karaoke, and that is where inactivity, and perhaps a touch of loneliness, leads us, monsieur

It wouldn't bother me to be a grandmother

Not of a shedload of kids, like poor Giselle

But of one little tot, who'd just be there

Though it makes no sense to bring people into the world these days

When I saw her again, poor Gigi had five grandchildren. Five…And a sixth when Corinna adopted the Vietnamese kid

After her days as a juvenile delinquent, Corinna turned Catholic, monsieur. She married a former sailor, who worked in marine insurance and gave her four kids, to which they added a Vietnamese boy

At the burial service, she wore a culotte skirt

As for Lola, she was pregnant at twenty by an unknown father, like her mother

I don't know if anyone has told you, madame, but in thirty years, the population of India (and I've come to think the Indians are sneakier than the Chinese) will be two billion

According to my son, when our poor planet Earth is completely swamped and overpopulated, man will sally forth to colonize other planets

This is a boy who has read *Forbes* since he was fourteen. He could tell you the amounts in dollars of the greatest fortunes in the world, and to whom they belonged, from the age of fourteen. My husband thought it was a positive sign for the future, and congratulated himself. The kid thinks big, he'd say

Now he also thinks *far*. He'd have no problem at all going to live on Mars. He sees nothing immoral in this every-man-for-himself business, because he's convinced we are a superior species

He thinks that human beings will adapt very well to life on Mars, or some other planet, the same way they adapted to rush hour on the ring road at six in the evening, which, he says, for men in the Middle Ages would have been a vision of the Apocalypse. What's more, he claims that without knowing it, and despite my lyrical outbursts on ecology, I'm adapting admirably well to the disappearance of hedgehogs, the extinction of sperm whales, dragonflies, earthworms, and wild rabbits because humans adapt to everything, absolutely everything

I don't like him

He's a hollow man

Even if he is right, I see nothing positive about being infinitely adaptable

Not far from where we lived in Saint-Sourd there was a little forest on a hill. In winter the ground was completely covered in leaves. If you dug down, there were even more leaves, a hill of leaves

In March we saw one or two wildflowers poke through

Then one day, there were no more leaves. We don't know where they went

I don't believe in God. But sometimes I pray to him under my breath

Or let's just say I try. I always start with, I know this isn't your concern, I know my request is minor and you have other things to do . . .

The moment I finish my intro, I stop, because it's obvious that he has other things to do

After my knee surgery, I was in so much pain that I gave the inner voice a try. Silent prayer, on the Q.T., soul to soul, you might say

At the funeral, where I went dragging my feet, Corinna wore a culotte skirt

A ladies'-church-auxiliary-style knee length corduroy culotte skirt

Gigi had always condemned culotte skirts. She put up with Corinna's electronic bracelet but the culotte skirt, no

I found it infinitely sad, monsieur, that on the day of the funeral, the woman wore a garment famously criticized by her mother

Everything eternally repeats itself. When we were young, we spat on religion. We thought we were done with that old bill of goods

Now we have to get back down on our knees

Ever since the fanatics, people have doted on the nice religious type. Who, in my opinion, has never been nice, and Gigi agreed. I don't know why they gave her a funeral Mass. On the other hand, it brought people out. It drew a few celebrities, Giselle would have been happy

When one is no longer belle of the ball, mademoiselle, one is quick to feel forgotten

The ceremony was at eleven o'clock at St. Barberine. My son came to pick me up at ten. That's how it is with us. We're the first to arrive and stand in the wind with worried faces, watching for the motorcade. There were gawkers, photographers—no great pomp, but a bit of hoopla all the same

We saw Anaïs Weber, and Jean-Louis Grozier and José Valadi, of course, climbing out of cars. I thought we'd see Alain Delon, but he didn't show. We saw Félix Jarreau, who had just lost his wife. She wrote god-awful plays that no one performed. On her deathbed, she summoned all her "friends," read: celebrities she'd never managed to hobnob with in life

The secretary of state for culture arrived wearing a mask of affliction. I'd have thought the minister herself would make a point of being there, madame, seeing as she'd made Gigi a Commander of the Order of Arts and Letters. Giselle showed me the official letter with a handwritten note from the minister, saying what a great personal honor it was to present her with this grade, the highest of the four distinctions awarded by the government of the French Republic, as Gigi repeated for days, reveling in the word *commander*. And though there was no obligation, she even thought of arranging an official presentation of the medal, until she learned you had to buy it yourself at the cost of five hundred and forty-five euros, at which point she said they could stick their medal where the sun doesn't shine

All those people, with their looks of devastation, had let Gigi go to rack and ruin, alone on rue de Courcelles

Who ever came to visit her?

Not much of anyone. Nobody important. Underlings. Florists' deliverymen who brought the bouquets she sent herself, like Marie Bell*

One night I slept at her place. At six a.m., I heard her yank the toilet-seat riser from the bowl. Gigi had to be

---

* A French tragedian, comic actor, and stage director (1900–1985). During the Occupation, she was one of the nine Résistance directors. From 1962 onward she directed the Théâtre du Gymnase in Paris, which now bears her name.

elevated because she had wrecked her back. At the age of seventy-one, she had gone out in the snow with six-inch heels, slipped, and gotten all smashed up. She put the toilet-seat riser in a ripped bag from La Forêt and, with all her might, threw it on top of the wardrobe. She did this on weekdays so that no one could see that she shat six feet above ground. In the evening, the maid fit it back over the toilet bowl before she went home

In Saint-Sourd, until my father's mother died, my sister and I went to hear the Mass in Latin every Sunday. I understood bugger-all. I only grasped that the soul was an organ that could not be put on the same level as a regular organ in the body. I pictured a fluttering, shimmery lung. In ads for poultices to relieve congestion, there was a fire-breathing faun clutching a phosphorescent cushion to its breast

For me, the soul was like that

Giselle's funeral Mass was celebrated by a Congolese priest. A double handicap for a deaf person, the echo from the mike in the church and the unintelligible accent. I'm a tad deaf. But I caught bits and pieces of it, madame

In a voice that plunged into a bottomless abyss, a voice that would never be allowed onstage, the priest exhorted us to rejoice and make our hearts glad, because, and I quote, Giselle practiced her faith in a spirit of caring for others

I looked around. No one to share that with, damn!

Next, standing before a big Warhol-esque portrait of Giselle, a woman sang Thérèse de Lisieux's *To Live on Love*, and I started to cry. You can't help yourself, it's the organ, it really gets you down. I pictured the dressing room and the fag in her mouth, and the hair, and the letters from her lovers, and little Kikine on the flowery daybed, Kikine who turned into that other person, stiff as a ramrod, in a culotte skirt

A thousand years that flashed by in a second

We bumped into each other on rue de Courcelles, almost right in front of her door. It was years after *Break of Noon*. Both of us were dazzled to be living in the same neighborhood. Come in, come up!

She lived alone in her big flat with decorative moldings

It was a cozy impersonal flat. There was one just like it on every floor of the building. No trace of the mess she used to make wherever she went, back when I knew her

She showed me her sideways view of Parc Monceau. A faint odor of camphor clung to the place

Giselle still appeared in films and TV series. She'd even returned to stage not long before

But the lights had gone cold, madame

We pretended not to notice. She served me a cup of tea. We went into raptures over the teacups she had bought for a euro at Hema. She brought out a picture of us that she had kept, taken at the entrance of the Théâtre de Clichy. I realized how beautiful she had been. I had a leering smile that I'd meant to be penetrating. Everyone knows how to make a photo-face but me. I told her I was widowed. My husband had died six months before. She asked me if his ghost ever visited. Gigi believed in ghosts. She told me that Ingmar Bergman's ghost came to her flat on a regular basis. They had long talks. About fate, pendulums, night, and tranquilizers, Gigi said, but also home decorating. —For example it was he who convinced me to change the kitchen tiles

Giselle thought it was a shame that he'd had his teeth redone and no longer had his pointy little incisor. I said, but when would he have had his teeth done? She did not know

I was happy to see her again, mademoiselle

As she spoke, she leaned her head back on the sofa, her feet up on the coffee table. I had forgotten this capacity for languor

On the street she'd seemed smaller than before. And she continued to seem smaller, right until her death

The Congolese priest made a gesture. Gigi's six grandchildren, necktied and squeezed into dark-colored suits, climbed onto the tiny podium. The eldest, a boy of about fifteen, whose voice was changing, read a text he'd written himself, which began, *Mamita, you've left us* . . . That was Giselle's grandma-name

Just what we needed, a remembrance of Giselle as Mamita, next to her psychedelic turquoise portrait!

Giselle had just wanted to be called Giselle, she had told me, but no one else agreed

Giselle equated "Mamita" with underarm flab, deafness, an uncooperative back, unruly bowels, quick fixes for the skin, muscles, and hair color, the whole torrent of ruin that hurls you into the arms of death before you know it

Gigi did not like old age

Who does?

In the end, she complained about everything, monsieur

About her entourage, her decrepitude, and especially her daughters, the youngest of whom showed her no affection. Gigi said, she kisses me through gritted teeth, as though my mouth were smeared with manure

When Raymond Lice started rambling, we worked out a system, we'd say "ding-dong!" each time he repeated himself

It worked like a charm

When he heard "ding-dong" he'd say, oh pardon me!

One day I dared to say, Gigi, remember Raymond and ding-dong? —Yes of course. —Well, each time you complain I'm going to say "ding-dong"

Do as you please

Corinna, in a surge of family feeling, had taken Gigi on holiday to Roquebrune. Holidays with the husband and the passel of brats. She called me every day

I hate ruins

I hate people who visit ruins

I hate the seaside

I hate children and their squealing joy. The Vietnamese kid is the worst. A cretin. Just because he's an adopted Vietnamese kid doesn't mean he's not a cretin

The priestling is a pain in the ass. The priestling is her son-in-law

The car is a pain in the ass

The Super U Mart is a pain in the ass

Ding-dong!

You're lucky to have a son, Anne-Marie, girls are nothing but hatred and resentment. I told the gastroenterologist that it's my morning orange juice that blocks my pylorus, but he couldn't care less, he wants me to take a double dose of Colopeg before the next colonoscopy, he says the last one must not have been done in the right conditions. I said, doc, you need your head examined. I'll go on a bulk-free diet for two weeks and it'll be spick and span in there, the way you want it. Ding-dong! I won't let you tear my innards to shreds because you take me for a half-wit! Ding-dong! You know, Anne-Marie, my left arm has been half-dead for months, I can't button a blouse anymore. The physio says that only the head should rest on the pillow, not the neck, I said we do the best we can to sleep, Monsieur Grenier, it's a miracle if we sleep at all, and then he said, well, don't be surprised if you end up with ankylosis. Oh, they're such a pain in the ass! Ding-dong ding-dong!

Well, it worked with Raymond Lice

Raymond ended his days in a state nursing home in Évry. I went to visit him once. He sat in a big yellow armchair next to his bed. The bed was in the middle of the room with the headboard pushed against the wall, like in the hospital

He did not remember my name. The in-house hair-dresser had given him a side part and crimped forelock like a little boy's

Raymond Lice, Canella Poupi, Mirelle Camp, Giselle Fayolle

My friends from Clichy

We had the time of our lives, you know

When I was little, for the holidays I was sent to stay with cousins on my mother's side. They put me on the train, I got off at Bluzet. I waited on the platform with my suitcase until my uncle finished work. He was the sta-tionmaster. In the summer, I poked around the shrubs behind the station and in the waiting room, which was empty, because usually only freight trains stopped there. I pined away from loneliness and boredom. My suitcase was packed with toiletries and easy-wash clothes. My mother folded everything very carefully to make a good impression

When I came to Paris, I wanted to bring things that mattered. Boxes of trinkets, notebooks, my album, pictures to hang, my papier-mâché animals

It was sad, monsieur, that trousseau for the unknown

Before rue des Rondeaux, I drifted right and left with a huge suitcase that I never unpacked

At rue des Rondeaux, I ditched almost everything

When Giselle died, you see, it's as if I unpacked my bag for the last time

When we came out of the church, it was raining. The men who had lowered the coffin were soaked

It rained at my father's funeral also

My parents were buried in the Mille family plot at the Colugne communal cemetery, which is smaller than Saint-Sourd's and gives onto a field

My father was first. We were all there in the pouring rain, my husband, my sister, my brother-in-law, more distant family, local residents, and old workers from the foundry. My mother was dressed like a Spanish lady with a black lace mantilla

She refused to carry an umbrella. She stood there stiff and chilled to the bone. The veil stuck to her streaming cheeks with an effect of embarrassing excess

There weren't as many people at hers. A few relatives, the cousins from Bluzet, minus the stationmaster, who had died long ago. My mother kept up her antics right until the end. A neighbor said she'd seen her cavorting down rue Carmelin not long before

As we left, we passed a grave heaped with fresh flowers. I looked at the name, and who do you think was buried there?

Who, mademoiselle? Prosper Ginot!

Prosper Ginot. One thousand nine hundred and eighteen — One thousand nine hundred and eighty-nine

Actor

Prosper Ginot, lying in the dark in Colugne next to my parents, facing a meadow full of cows and poppies

Where I come from, lying down is not allowed

The recumbent position is bad for the soul

In Saint-Sourd, there were the coal pits which no longer exist and the Prosper Ginot theater company

We saw the actors around town, especially on Sundays, on account of the market

I recognized them from afar

I whispered their names

Prosper Ginot, Armand Cheval . . .

They were tall and pale. Much larger than life

We told ourselves that our lives were very small

No artist has ever been as grand as the actors of Saint-Sourd-en-Ger

Prosper Ginot, Madeleine Puglierin, Roger Stru, Madeleine Tison, Armand Cheval, Désiré Guelde, Odette Ordonneau, Aimé Morteron, Jean Leleu, Georgia Glazer

ABOUT THE AUTHOR

Yasmina Reza is a novelist and playwright. Her plays *Conversations After a Burial*, *The Unexpected Man*, *Art*, *Life x 3*, and *God of Carnage* have all been multi-award-winning critical and popular international successes, translated into more than thirty-five languages. *Art* was the first non-English language play to win the American Tony Award. *God of Carnage*, which also won a Tony Award, was adapted for film in 2012 by Roman Polanski. Her novels include *Babylon* (Seven Stories, 2018), which won the Prix Renaudot and was shortlisted for the Prix Goncourt; *Desolation*; and *Adam Haberberg*. *Anne-Marie the Beauty* is her most recent novel. She lives in Paris.

ABOUT THE TRANSLATOR

Alison L. Strayer is a Canadian writer and translator. She won the Warwick Prize for Women in Translation, and her work has been shortlisted for the Governor General's Award for Literature and for Translation, the Grand Prix du livre de Montreal, the Prix littéraire France-Québec, and the Man Booker International Prize. She lives in Paris.

ABOUT SEVEN STORIES PRESS

Seven Stories Press is an independent book publisher based in New York City. We publish works of the imagination by such writers as Nelson Algren, Russell Banks, Octavia E. Butler, Ani DiFranco, Assia Djebar, Ariel Dorfman, Coco Fusco, Barry Gifford, Martha Long, Luis Negrón, Peter Plate, Hwang Sok-yong, Lee Stringer, and Kurt Vonnegut, to name a few, together with political titles by voices of conscience, including Subhankar Banerjee, the Boston Women's Health Collective, Noam Chomsky, Angela Y. Davis, Human Rights Watch, Derrick Jensen, Ralph Nader, Loretta Napoleoni, Gary Null, Greg Palast, Project Censored, Barbara Seaman, Alice Walker, Gary Webb, and Howard Zinn, among many others. Seven Stories Press believes publishers have a special responsibility to defend free speech and human rights, and to celebrate the gifts of the human imagination, wherever we can. In 2012 we launched Triangle Square books for young readers with strong social justice and narrative components, telling personal stories of courage and commitment. For additional information, visit www.sevenstories.com.